What Will I Be?

A Wish Book

by Kathleen Krull Cowles
illustrated by Eulala Conner

GOLDEN PRESS
Western Publishing Company, Inc.
Racine, Wisconsin

Second Printing, 1980

Most boys and girls have special daydreams and wishes about what they'd like to do and what they'd like to be. What is your special wish?

Sometimes I daydream about taking the fastest bicycle ride ever. I'll invite all of my friends to ride along with me, and we'll see who gets to the top of the hill first.

Then we'll race to the bottom of the hill!

When I get bigger, I'd like to be a baker like Joe in the bakery. The cakes I make will always have at least eight layers —

with gooey chocolate frosting
(or maybe peanut butter!)
in between the layers.

I wonder what it would be like to be a bricklayer when I grow up. I love to build things, so I think I'd have fun making buildings. I'd be very careful to lay each brick close to the one before. But I'd always leave an opening toward the top of the tower, so my fairy princess doll could look outside.

When I grow up, I'll like people to call me up on the telephone every time they need a friend.

I'll make them laugh if they feel sad. And if they want someone to listen to their jokes, *I'll* laugh for *them*.

I think I'll be a famous fire fighter when I grow up, because I know what an important job it is to protect people from fires. Everyone in my neighborhood will be safe whenever I'm on the job.

I wish I could have the biggest garden in the world. M-m-m-m! I'm getting so hungry just thinking about it!

When I'm older, I'd like to be a librarian in a children's library. I could be the first to read all those good books, and I could help my friends find the books they'd like.

When I grow up, I want to learn how to fix cars. My own special cars will always be red sports cars, but maybe I'll fix other kinds, too.

When I get bigger, I'm going to the North Pole to make lots of snowthings. I love to make snowmen, but they always melt too fast where I live!

My favorite daydream is to join the circus and become its star dancer. I'll be able to dance on horses — and maybe on elephants, too, if they promise not to jiggle around.

Someday I'd like to be a bug. Not a scary
kind of bug, but just a crawly, friendly bug —
the kind of bug that would tickle my big sister
with its feet.

When I'm older, I'm going to write monster stories. I'll have to try not to scare myself too much, but I'll sure scare the people who read my stories!

When I get just a little bigger, I'm going to be a champion swimmer. I'll win all of the contests in the shallow end —

and even some of the contests in the deep end!

More than anything else, I wish I could become a great mountain climber. I'd take my pet
goat along for company. The tallest mountain
wouldn't be too high for us to climb!

Someday I'm going to learn how to make up my own jigsaw puzzles. My friends will think I'm the fastest puzzle-solver around!

Boy, will my piano teacher be surprised when I become a famous pianist! I'll travel all over the world giving free concerts, and everyone, especially my teacher, will clap for me.

When I grow up, maybe I'll be a plant doctor.
Lots of my friends will have sick plants, and I'll
know all about how to make them well.

What would it be like to be a train engineer when I grow up? I bet all the people would watch for me and wave. My train would be an especially big one — just for me!

When I grow up, I hope I can be a grandpa. Then my grandchildren will always come and tell me what *they* want to be when they grow up. And I'll smile and tell them, "Of course! You can be practically whatever you want to be if you just make up your mind to it — so wish away!"